W9-AJU-414

COUNTING AMERICA

The Story of the United States Census

COUNTING
AMERICA

The Story of the United States Census

Melissa Ashabranner

Brent Ashabranner

G. P. Putnam's Sons • *New York*

Designed by Joy Taylor

Library of Congress Cataloging-in-Publication Data
Ashabranner, Melissa. Counting America:
the story of the United States census /
Melissa Ashabranner and Brent Ashabranner.
p.   cm. Bibliography: p.   Summary: Traces history of
the population census and describes how
and why information about the number and characteristics of the
people living in the United States is gathered every ten years.
ISBN 0-399-21747-9
1. United States—Census.   [1. United States—Census.]
I. Ashabranner, Brent K., 1921–   . II. Title.
HA37.U55A78   1989   304.6′0723—dc19   88–37572   CIP   AC

1 3 5 7 9 10 8 6 4 2
First Impression

CONTENTS

For
Giancarlo Brent Fagon
A boy of the twenty-first century

ACKNOWLEDGMENTS

WE WOULD like to thank the following staff members of the Bureau of the Census for providing us with information and patiently answering our questions about the Census of Population and Housing that is conducted in the United States once in every decade. Their friendly and thoughtful help made our work on this book a pleasure: Peter Bounpane, Assistant Director for Decennial Census; Cheryl Chambers, Public Affairs Specialist; Deborah Harner, Branch Chief, Census Evaluation; Charles D. Jones, Associate Director for Decennial Census; Robert A. LaMacchia, Assistant Division Chief for Planning, Geography Division; Mark Mangold, Public Affairs Specialist; Stanley D. Matchett, Chief, Field Division; Susan M. Miskura, Chief, Decennial Planning Division; Jerry Potosky, Field Representative; and former Census Bureau Regional Director for Field Operations, Richard Schweitzer.

We also would like to express our appreciation to Richard E. Shute, Director for Management and Information Systems, Department of Commerce, for pointing us in the right direction at the beginning of our research and to Stephen J. Tordella, General Manager of Decision Demographics, Population Reference Bureau, for valuable insights into private sector use of census information.

Melissa Ashabranner
Brent Ashabranner

COUNTING AMERICA

The Story of the United States Census

★ ONE ★

THE CENSUS

Taking a Picture of America

WHO are we? What do we really look like as a nation? How many people who live in the United States are white? How many are black? How many are of Asian or Spanish origin? How many are American Indians? Where do all these people live? What kind of work do they do? How much education do they have? What kind of houses do they live in? What is the size of an average household? How many people in the country are poor? Why are they poor?

Every ten years the federal government makes a huge effort to answer all of these questions and many others about the people who live in the United States. This gigantic task is called a census of population: counting every person who lives within the borders of the nation and gathering information about them.

The United States—and every other modern country—must have reliable and up-to-date information about its people in order to carry out the business of government at every level: national, state,

This special clock at the Census Bureau shows how America's population grows by one person every 17 seconds. On Census Day in 1990 the clock is expected to read at least 250,000,000.

★ ★ ★ ★ ★

county, and city. We need to know how many children there are, how old they are, and where they live, so that the right number of schools can be built in the right places. We need to know what parts of the country are growing fastest in population in order to plan for future roads, gas and electrical power, and telephone service. Information about areas of poverty and bad housing will help focus programs of government assistance where they are most needed. These are but a few of the hundreds of uses that census information is put to every day.

The census is really a picture of America—a statistical or numerical picture—that tells us what we look like as a nation at a particular moment in history. The picture is taken by the Census Bureau, which is a part of the U. S. Department of Commerce, and it is taken in every year that ends in zero. The last census of the United States was taken in 1980; the next will be taken in 1990.

The Census and the Constitution

We take a population census of the United States every ten years for another reason, and it is the most important reason of all. In 1787 delegates from each of the states met in a Constitutional Convention to try to draft a Constitution that would take the place of the old Articles of Confederation. While they agreed on many things, delegates from the large and small states hotly debated the question of how their states would be represented in the new government. Under one proposal, supported by the large states, representation would be determined by population alone, making the small states much less powerful. The argument became so bitter that the small states threatened to leave the convention. If that had happened, there might never have been a United States.

But in a crucial compromise the delegates agreed that Congress would be m ide up of two bodies. One would be the Senate, and each state woulc be allowed two senators, regardless of the state's population. The other body of Congress would be the House of Representatives, and the number of representatives from each state would be based on the number of people who lived in the state. Thus, a heavily populated state like New York or Pennsylvania would have a large number of representatives, while a small state like Rhode Island or Delaware would have only a few, but at least one.

The Founding Fathers realized that the compromise would work only if the population of each state could be determined accurately. They also saw that state populations would have to be rechecked at regular intervals in the future because change was certain. To solve this problem, the drafters of the Constitution wrote into the first article a requirement for a national census that would count the inhabitants of each state.

Article I, section 2, of the Constitution reads: "Representatives . . . shall be apportioned among the several States which may be included within this Union according to their respective Numbers. . . . The actual enumeration shall be made within three Years after the first Meeting of the Congress of the United States, and within every subsequent Term of ten Years. . . ."

The Constitution was adopted by the states in 1789, and the first census was taken in 1790. A census has been taken every ten years since that time.

But once the issue of representation based on population had been settled, another issue arose, this time between the slave-owning states in the South and the northern states. Under the new Constitution, states would be taxed based on the size of their population, just as their entitlement to seats in the House of Representatives would be based on population. The southern states, which had thousands of slaves, wanted the slaves to be counted as less than free persons for taxation purposes. The delegates from the North said that slaves should count the same as free persons for taxation; they should count less, however, when it came to apportioning representatives for Congress.

Some said slaves should not be counted at all because they were "property." Others said they should be counted equally with free

Susan Miskura, Director of the Decennial Planning Division for the 1990 census. She first became interested in the census after reading about it in My Weekly Reader *when she was twelve years old. After she graduated with a degree in statistics from the University of Rochester, she joined the Census Bureau.*

★ ★ ★ ★ ★

All members of a household born before Census Day must be included when filling out the form.

The arrival of the census taker could be an exciting event for people living in remote settlements in the early days of the United States. This drawing is from an early issue of Harper's Weekly.

persons. In the end another compromise was reached. The decision was that for both direct taxation and representation, slaves would count three-fifths as much as free persons. Thus, for example, a thousand slaves would be equivalent to six hundred free persons. Only a bitter war between the North and South would provide the final solution to this tragic problem.

Early Censuses in History

The United States is the first country in history to take a census regularly from its very beginning as a nation. It is by no means, however, the first country to take a census. Censuses of all or some part of a country's population have been taken for almost as long as people have lived under governments. Early population counts were made in China and Japan; and censuses were taken by the ancient Babylonians, Egyptians, Greeks, and Romans.

A number of censuses are reported in the Bible. In the Second Book of Samuel, Chapter 24, Verse 2, King David instructs Joab: "Go now through all the tribes of Israel, from Dan even to Beer-sheba, and number ye the people, that I may know the number of the people." Chapter 1 of the Book of Numbers is a detailed description of a census that was taken to determine the number of men in Israel available to fight in war.

Censuses in ancient times were almost entirely for the purpose of finding out how many men were available for military service and for determining the number and location of households that could be taxed. Indeed, the word "census" comes from the Latin word *censere*, which means "to tax." Is it any wonder that census takers in those early days were feared and resented and that people tried to avoid them?

Beginning in the mid-eighteenth century, some European countries—Sweden, Norway, Denmark—undertook complete population counts at regular intervals. These probably were the first modern censuses in that the results were used not only for determining taxation and military service but also for helping to assess educational, commercial, and other needs. Although the purpose of modern censuses is to provide governments with information that will help the people of their country, suspicion of censuses remains a problem for census takers to this day.

★ TWO ★

DEVELOPMENT OF THE
U. S. CENSUS

THE first enumeration or population census of the United States was a hit-or-miss effort at best. The pioneering task was entrusted to sixteen federal marshals, one for each of the thirteen states and three territories that existed in 1790. The states were Connecticut, Delaware, Georgia, Maryland, Massachusetts, New Hampshire, New Jersey, New York, North Carolina, Pennsylvania, Rhode Island, South Carolina, and Virginia. The territories were Kentucky, Maine, and Vermont. The marshals had a total of two hundred assistants, who did most of the work.

The enumerators, as the assistants were called, had no experience or training. They had no questionnaire forms to work with. Each marshal bought notebooks or paper for his assistants, and all sizes and shapes of paper were used, making the final tabulation of figures difficult. These original "census forms" are stored at the National Archives in Washington, D. C., and can be seen on microfilm.

The Return for SOUTH CAROLINA having been made fince the foregoing Schedule was originally printed, the whole Enumeration is here given complete, except for the N. Weftern Territory, of which no Return has yet been publifhed.

DISTICTS	Free white Males of 16 years and upwards, including heads of families.	Free white Males under sixteen years.	Free white Females, including heads of families.	All other free persons.	Slaves.	Total.
Vermont	22435	22328	40505	255	16	85539
N. Hampfhire	36086	34851	70160	630	158	141885
Maine	24384	24748	46870	538	NONE	96540
Maffachufetts	95453	87289	190582	5463	NONE	378787
Rhode Ifland	16019	15799	32652	3407	948	68825
Connecticut	60523	54403	117448	2808	2764	237946
New York	83700	78122	152320	4654	21324	340120
New Jerfey	45251	41416	83287	2762	11423	184139
Pennfylvania	110788	106948	206363	6537	3737	434373
Delaware	11783	12143	22384	3899	8887	59094
Maryland	55915	51339	101395	8043	103036	319728
Virginia	110936	116135	215046	12866	292627	747610
Kentucky	15154	17057	28922	114	12430	73677
N. Carolina	69988	77556	140710	4975	100572	393751
S. Carolina	35576	37722	66880	1801	107094	249073
Georgia	13103	14044	25739	398	29264	82548
	807094	791850	1541263	59150	694280	3893635

Total number of Inhabitants of the United States exclufive of S. Weftern and N. Territory.	Free white Males of 21 years and upwards.	Free Males under 21 years of age.	Free white Females.	All other Perfons.	Slaves.	Total
S. W. territory	6271	10277	15365	361	3417	35691
N. Ditto	—	—	—	—	—	—

Official report of the 1790 census, the first counting of America.

But problems of recording and tabulating answers were small compared to the problems of collecting information. Ninety-five percent of the population of the country at that time lived in rural areas, mostly on isolated farms and plantations that had to be visited on horseback or on foot. The few roads that existed were in poor condition. Rivers had to be forded because there were few bridges. Detailed maps were only a hope of the future. For the most part enumerators had to go out and simply learn by word of mouth where households might be located in the vast wilderness that was America in the years following the Revolutionary War.

Even when a household was located, the enumerator's problems were often far from over. Most of the people that the enumerators interviewed had no idea why the census was being taken. The question about slaves sounded as if it might be for taxation; the question about males sixteen and older seemed to be seeking information that could be used for military service. Some people ran when they saw the enumerator coming. Some refused to answer the questions, although they could be fined for not answering. In some cases census takers were attacked and even tarred and feathered.

Yet the first census was taken. It was supposed to have been completed in nine months but took eighteen. When the final tabulation was made in early March, 1792, Thomas Jefferson, who was in charge of the enumeration, sent a copy of the census to President George Washington. According to the final count, the population of the United States, at the outset of nationhood, was 3,929,326.

Jefferson knew that not everyone had been counted; he estimated that the total population was above four million, probably close to 4,100,000. Washington shared Jefferson's belief that the count was incomplete; he blamed people who concealed information because they thought the census was for taxation. Washington also put blame on some enumerators for what he called "want of activity," by which he meant laziness. Nevertheless, Washington thought the first U. S. census was better than any census ever taken in Europe

Henry Kline	Shopkeeper	260	d		1	4	1
	(Vac) 262	264				
	do	266	s			
Henry Kream	Shopkeeper	268	a		2		1
	Vac	270				
Joseph Ogden	Flk Market	270	d		6		3
William Lowman	Rope Mast.	272	a		1	4	2
Reuben New Houses	Vac 274	274	d				
	Vacant	276				
William Hamilton	Ho Carpr	280	d		1		2
Remainder Vacant to Ninth Street						
Van Berkel minister from the Netherlands	Amount over			2226	1519	3966
Tho. Jefferson Sec. of State	do the US					
Edmund Randolph Atty Gen of the US						

Thomas Jefferson, Secretary of State; Edmond Randolph, Attorney
General; and Van Berkal, Minister from the Netherlands, added their
names to a Philadelphia census register.
Courtesy: Archives of the United States.

★ ★ ★ ★ ★

and that it would impress on European leaders the "growing importance" of the United States.

The Growing Need for Information

Besides counting the number of free persons and slaves in the various states and territories, the first census determined head of household, sex of free persons, and age of white males over sixteen. Even before the census of 1790 was taken, however, some members of the first Congress urged that the census be used to collect other facts. The Union was just beginning. The fledgling government knew almost nothing about the people of the new nation. Without information how could Congress and the President make decisions and pass laws that were in the people's best interests?

James Madison, when he was a member of the first Congress, was one of those who saw the nation's need for more information. He proposed that the first census determine the age of every free person and that the occupations of all employed persons be recorded. But other members of Congress felt that collecting additional information would cost too much and take too much time. Others believed that gathering information about individuals beyond that needed to determine representatives for Congress was an invasion of privacy. Therefore, the second census, taken in 1800, asked only the same questions as the first census.

Very quickly, however, both government and the private sector realized that accurate, up-to-date information was necessary to run the country and carry out its business. From the time of the 1810 census—when Madison was President—information gathering, beyond the population head count, became an important part of the census.

One of the most important changes took place in 1850. Before that time, only the name of the head of the household had been taken. Beginning in 1850, the name of every person was recorded,

THE GREAT TRIBULATION.

CENSUS MARSHAL.—"I jist want to know how many of yez is deaf, dumb, blind, insane and idiotic—likewise how many convicts there is in the family—what all your ages are, especially the old woman and the young ladies—and how many dollars the old gentleman is worth!"

[Tremendous sensation all round the table.]

This cartoon from an 1866 Saturday Evening Post *ridicules the overinquisitive census taker. But society's need for information versus the individual's right to privacy has always been a serious concern of census officials.*

together with his or her age, marital status, and race or nationality. Questions have changed from census to census, but some important and long-lasting ones have sought to determine education, occupation, place of birth, employment status, income, type of housing, and condition of housing.

One piece of information, however, ceased to be needed. The last counting of slaves in America was the census of 1860. By 1870 the Civil War had been fought, and slavery in America was a thing of the past.

Changes in Taking the Census

While the gathering of different kinds of information grew rapidly, changes in methods of census taking came more slowly. Uniform census questionnaires were not printed until 1830. It was not until 1880 that specially appointed and trained census supervisors and enumerators replaced federal marshals and assistant marshals as census takers. From 1790 through 1900 there was no permanent census office. It was disbanded after each census was taken and the results processed. Only in 1902 did Congress establish a permanent Bureau of the Census (usually referred to as the Census Bureau) with a permanent staff; this new bureau became a part of the Department of Commerce. Today the Census Bureau is headquartered in the Washington, D. C., suburb of Suitland, Maryland, with regional offices in many parts of the country.

A crucial change in gathering census information took place in 1960. For the first time census questionnaires were mailed through the post office to most of the households in the United States with instructions that they were to be filled out and held until picked up by an enumerator. This was called self-enumeration, and the idea behind it was that the person in the household filling out the questionnaire would have more time to think about the answers. Also, a great deal of time and money would be saved since the Census

Bureau enumerator would have to help only those households that had trouble filling out the questionnaire.

Self-enumeration worked so well that in 1970 the Census Bureau began what it called the mail out/mail back method. The census questionnaire was mailed to almost all households with instructions to mail it back to the Census Bureau (in an envelope supplied by the Bureau) after it was filled out. Enumerators would go only to households which requested help, did not return the questionnaire, or filled it out incorrectly. The mail out/mail back method of self-enumeration was considered quite successful and was improved and used again in 1980. The Census Bureau will try to reach at least 95 percent of all American households with the mail out/mail back method in 1990.

The 1990 Decennial Census

The population census of the United States is called the "decennial" census, which means that it is the census taken every ten years. The word "decennial" distinguishes it from many other censuses and surveys the Census Bureau carries out every year. The 1990 decennial census will be America's bicentennial census—two hundred years of census taking in the United States without missing a single decennial year.

These censuses give us an accurate picture of how we have grown as a nation. There were just under 4 million people living in the United States at the time of the first census in 1790. By 1850 the population of the country had grown to 23 million. By 1900 it was 76 million; by 1950, 125 million. When the last decennial census was taken in 1980, the exact count of the U. S. population was 226,545,805. Estimations are that the population of the country will be about 250 million in 1990, but only the census will provide the official figure.

While our nation was growing, its people were on the move. At

In 1990, an estimated 106 million households in the United States will receive their census form by mail. They are asked to complete it and mail it back.

The Census Bureau employs almost 9,000 professionals, such as geographers, economists, cartographers, computer experts, and statisticians.

The Bureau of the Census is headquartered in Suitland, Maryland, in a vast office complex pictured in this aerial view.

the time of the first census in 1790, just 5 percent of the U. S. population lived in urban areas—places with at least 2,500 people. In 1980, 73 percent of all Americans—165 million people—lived in or near cities with a population of fifty thousand or more. Along with our urban growth went steady westward migration; such states as Texas, Arizona, and California are the fastest growing in the country. Our nation's many population shifts have been recorded by the decennial censuses.

The differences between the first census in 1790 and the bicentennial census in 1990 are almost unimaginable. The first census was taken by sixteen marshals and two hundred assistants. Despite self-enumeration, the 1990 census will require three hundred thousand enumerators and supervisors! Eighteen months were required to take the first census. Most of the 1990 census will be taken in one day and will be completed in a few weeks. The first census asked only five questions. The 1990 census will ask over sixty questions about age, race, nationality, education, income, type of housing, and much more. The first census was tabulated by hand. The data from the 1990 census will be processed by hundreds of machines and computers.

But despite the huge differences between the census of 1790 and the census of 1990, the fundamental purpose of census taking will remain the same: to count every person—every man, woman, and child—living in the United States.

★ THREE ★

GETTING READY FOR THE DECENNIAL CENSUS

Every year ending in zero has an official Census Day that is set by Congress. The first Census Day was the first Monday in August, 1790, and other dates were chosen as Census Day throughout the nineteenth and early twentieth centuries. Since 1930, however, Congress has set Census Day as April 1.

The decennial census is a count of everyone living in the United States *as of* April 1 of the year the census is taken. Census Day is, therefore, a cut-off day. A baby born on April 2, 1990, for example, would not be counted in the 1990 census. He would be counted in the decennial census taken in the year 2000. An immigrant arriving in the United States on May 1, 1990, would not be counted in the 1990 census statistics.

Within nine months after Census Day—by January 1—the Secretary of Commerce must report to the President the total population of the United States *by state* as of April 1 of the decennial census year. These figures will determine how many members of the House of Representatives each state will be entitled to.

Census Day is also important because it gives the Census Bureau a target date for getting ready to take the census. Most Americans are aware of the census for only a short time once every ten years. Many never think about it except when they receive and fill out their census questionnaire. They know nothing about the years of preparation that precede a decennial census.

The Bureau's Decennial Planning Division coordinates this preparation and works out a budget for the entire census process. The budget is prepared at the outset of the decennial period but can be adjusted later if necessary. It will include funds for developing, printing, and mailing the census questionnaire; salaries for all decennial staff, including the hundreds of thousands of enumerators; millions of dollars for equipment to process the completed census questionnaires; funds for analyzing the census results and publishing studies and reports containing census information. Money also must be budgeted for telling people about the importance of being counted in the census.

The budget for the 1990 decennial census is $2.6 billion. That seems like a great deal of money, and it is. With an estimated population in 1990 of 250 million, the cost breaks down to just over ten dollars for each person in the United States. The many important uses of census information make that cost seem reasonable.

Planning the Census Questionnaire

The decennial census must produce information that will meet the critical data needs of the United States for the next ten years; therefore, nothing in the entire census process is more important than asking the right questions on the census questionnaire. The desire for information in America knows no limits. Government officials, industry market specialists, and research social scientists have hundreds of questions they would like to ask in the census.

For the 1990 census, 450 temporary district offices must be leased and equipped. In 1980 the Bureau leased 4 million square feet of space and purchased 65,000 desks, 52,000 folding chairs, 4 million pencils, and 750,000 pocket-sized pencil sharpeners.

★ ★ ★ ★ ★

But space on the census questionnaire is limited, and most people will not fill out a questionnaire that is long and complicated. For these reasons the Census Bureau must develop a census questionnaire that is easy to complete and that yields the maximum amount of useful information without taking too long to fill out.

Actually, there are two census forms. One is a short form, which will go to almost 90 million households in the 1990 census. Besides the name of everyone in a household and how they are related, the short form asks the age, sex, race, ancestry or ethnic origin, and marital status of each person. It also asks a few questions about housing: whether the dwelling is a house or apartment, amount of rent or mortgage payment, number of rooms, value. The short form of the census questionnaire takes about fifteen minutes to fill out.

About one out of every six households will be enumerated on a long form of the census questionnaire, which takes an average of forty minutes to complete. The households that receive the long form are selected in such a way that the information collected will be representative of many households like them. This is a statistical method called sampling, at which the Census Bureau is very skilled.

The long form contains all of the questions asked on the short form. In addition, it asks questions about school enrollment, amount of education, occupation, income, citizenship, current language and English ability, disability or handicap in household, and much more.

The long form of the questionnaire also asks a number of questions about the housing unit itself: age of the house or apartment building, number of bedrooms, source of water, type of sewage disposal, heating equipment, kitchen facilities, whether there is a telephone, and more. Information about housing is very important. In fact, the official name of the decennial census is the Census of Population and Housing. Among many other things, the census identifies parts of the country where low-cost housing programs are needed.

The questionnaire used in the last census is always the basis for the questionnaire that will be used in an upcoming census. Most of the questions that appear on the 1980 census questionnaire, for

TOPICS TO BE COVERED BY THE 1990 CENSUS

POPULATION   HOUSING

Items Collected at Every Household

Household relationship
Sex
Race
Age
Marital status
Spanish/Hispanic origins

Number of units at address
House or apartment
Number of rooms
Whether own or rent
Whether unit is one-family house
Unit shared with business
Value of home
Rent
Whether rent includes meals

Items Collected at Every Sixth Household

State or country of birth
Citizenship
Date of immigration
School enrollment
Educational attainment
Ancestry and ethnic origin
Mobility
Current language and English
  proficiency
Veteran status and period of
  service
Presence of disability or
  handicap
Number of children ever born
Employment status last week
Hours worked last week
Place of work
Method of transportation to work
Persons in car pool
Travel time to work
Unemployment information
Industry worked in
Occupation class of worker
Work in 1989 and weeks looking
  for work in 1989
Amount and source of income in
  1989

Number of bedrooms
Complete plumbing
  facilities
Complete kitchen facilities
Telephone
Number of vehicles
Fuels used for house
Water source
Sewage disposal
Year built
Condominium status and fee
Acreage and crop sales
Utility payments
Real estate taxes
Insurance costs
Debt on property
Mortgage payments
Second mortgages and home
  equity loans
Mobile home

PERSON 1

Last name	First name	Middle initial

8. In what U.S. State or foreign country was this person born?

(Name of State or foreign country; or Puerto Rico, Guam, etc.)

9. Is this person a CITIZEN of the United States?

- ○ Yes, born in the United States — *Skip to 11*
- ○ Yes, born in Puerto Rico, Guam, the U.S. Virgin Islands, or Northern Marianas ■
- ○ Yes, born abroad of American parent or parents
- ○ Yes, U.S. citizen by naturalization
- ○ No, not a citizen of the United States

10. When did this person come to the United States to stay?

○ 1987 or 1988 ■	○ 1970 to 1974
○ 1985 or 1986	○ 1965 to 1969
○ 1982 to 1984	○ 1960 to 1964
○ 1980 or 1981	○ 1950 to 1959
○ 1975 to 1979	○ Before 1950

11. At any time since February 1, 1988, has this person attended regular school or college? *Include only nursery school, kindergarten, elementary school, and schooling which leads to a high school diploma or a college degree.*

- ○ No, has not attended since February 1.
- ○ Yes, public school, public college. ■
- ○ Yes, private school, private college.

12. How much school has this person COMPLETED? *Fill ONE circle for the highest level COMPLETED or degree RECEIVED. If currently enrolled, mark the level of previous grade attended or highest degree received.*

- ○ Never attended school
- ○ Nursery school
- ○ Kindergarten
- ○ 1st, 2nd, 3rd, or 4th grade ■
- ○ 5th, 6th, 7th, or 8th grade
- ○ 9th grade
- ○ 10th grade
- ○ 11th grade
- ○ 12th grade, **NO DIPLOMA**
- ○ **HIGH SCHOOL GRADUATE**— high school DIPLOMA or the equivalent *(for example: GED)*
- ○ Some college but no degree ■
- ○ Associate degree in college — *Occupational program*
- ○ Associate degree in college — *Academic program*
- ○ Bachelor's degree *(for example: BA, AB, BS)*
- ○ Master's degree *(for example: MA, MS, MEng, MEd, MSW, MBA)*

14a. Did this person live in this house or apartmen 5 years ago *(on March 20, 1983)?*

- ○ Born after March 20, 1983 — *Go to questions for the next person*
- ○ Yes — *Skip to 15*
- ○ No

b. Where did this person live 5 years ago (on March 20, 1983)?

(1) Name of U.S. State or foreign country

(If outside U.S., print answer above and skip to

(2) Name of county in the U.S.

(3) Name of city or town in the U.S.

(4) Did this person live inside the city or town limits?

- ○ Yes
- ○ No, lived outside the city/town limits

15a. Does this person speak a language other than English at home?

- ○ Yes
- ○ No — *Skip to question 1*

b. What is this language?

(for example: Chinese, Italian, Spanish, Vietname

c. How well does this person speak English?

○ Very well	○ Not well
○ Well	○ Not at all

16. When was this person born?

- ○ Born before March 20, 1973— *Go to 17-33*
- ○ Born March 20, 1973 or later — *Turn to next p for the next person*

■

17a. Has this person ever been on active-duty milit service in the Armed Forces of the United Sta or ever been in the United States military Res or the National Guard? *If service was in Reserve National Guard only, see instruction guide.*

- ○ Yes, now on active duty
- ○ Yes, on active duty in past, but not now
- ○ Yes, service in Reserves or National Guard only — *Skip to 18*
- ○ No — *Skip to 18*

b. Was active-duty military service during —

A committee concerned with questions about ethnic minorities discusses the 1990 census.

★　★　★　★　★

A page from the 1990 Census of Population and Housing.

example, will be repeated on the 1990 census questionnaire. Experience with the 1980 census proved that they yielded valuable information; in most cases, updated information of the same type—size of households, housing conditions, income, educational attainment—is what government planners and researchers need.

But every prospective census question—whether or not it has been used before—is studied, discussed, and tested before it is finally added to the questionnaire. Census Bureau staff in the Decennial Planning Division make the first selection of questions, but they are then submitted to a long review and testing process. To prepare for the 1990 census, the Census Bureau held sixty-five public meetings in major cities all over the United States to seek advice on census questionnaire content and to discuss proposed questions. These meetings were attended by state and local government officials, business men and women, educators, and researchers from many fields.

While these meetings were going on, the Census Bureau organized ten federal government interagency working groups to discuss the census questions; these groups dealt with census topics such as housing, health, transportation, income, and poverty. The Census Bureau also worked on the questionnaire with the Congressional oversight committees, and the specific questions chosen for the 1990 census were submitted to Congress, as required by law.

Finally, several test censuses are held in different parts of the country, not only to try out the questionnaire but also to sharpen the whole census operation—mail out/mail back, enumerator field work, publicizing the census, processing questionnaires. Test censuses were held in 1985, 1986, and 1987 in California, Florida, Mississippi, New Jersey, and North Dakota. A full-scale dress rehearsal for the 1990 census was held on March 20, 1988, in Saint Louis and Columbia, Missouri, and in rural counties in the state of Washington. This dress rehearsal reached almost half a million households.

The residents of test areas are informed that the Census Bureau will be trying out various procedures. The Bureau emphasizes, how-

To promote participation in the census, the Census Bureau sponsors poster contests among schoolchildren.

During prelist operations, enumerators visit buildings that appear vacant at least twice, to make sure no one is living there.

ever, that the information collected is official; it will benefit the areas selected by providing current population totals and other data.

With the work of the Census Bureau staff, public meetings, inter-agency government working groups, Congressional oversight, and testing, the census questionnaire that finally emerges is probably the most carefully prepared document in the world.

Hunting Households

How do you find 250 million people in a country that stretches from the Atlantic to the Pacific and far beyond to Alaska and Hawaii? The Census Bureau's answer to that question is to create a huge address list of all the places that people live. According to Charles Jones, Associate Director for the 1990 Decennial Census, an accurate address list is the key to a successful census.

The creation of this list begins with the purchase of sixty million addresses, mostly in urban areas, from companies that sell current mailing lists for commercial purposes. Thirty million addresses will be added to this list in an operation known as "prelist." Prelist enu-merators are sent into rural areas to update previous census address lists for these areas.

This master list of ninety million addresses is then given to the United States Postal Service to conduct an Advance Post Office Check. Each mail carrier checks the list for his or her route, adds any addresses that are missing, and removes any addresses that no longer exist. If an apartment building has been torn down, the mail carrier will indicate that no census forms should be sent to the addresses that used to be in that building. If a new house has been built, the carrier will add its address to the list. When the Post Office has finished this advance check, the Census Bureau's master list will be about 95 percent complete.

But this still is not good enough. A year before the decennial census is taken, the Census Bureau will send teams of enumerators to carry out a "precanvass." In precanvass, enumerators travel every street and road in the United States to make sure that all the houses or places where a person could live are on the address list for the area they are checking.

They carry with them a map with only features such as streets, rivers, railroads, and lakes indicated on it. If they find a dwelling that is not on their address list, they must show its location on the map. These maps are then sent to Census Bureau headquarters, and the new address is put into the computer so that it will appear on future address lists. Precanvass enumerators find about 85 percent of all places that are still missing from the master address list. This makes the list 98 percent complete.

On March 28, 1990—three days before Census Day—the Census Bureau will mail out census questionnaires to approximately 106 million households in the United States. Finding the 2 percent of the households missing from the master list will be the task of the three hundred thousand enumerators who will begin their work after Census Day.

Telling People about the Census

"You can't force people to be counted."

That statement by Vincent P. Barabba, former Director of the Census Bureau, is true. Even though federal law requires that people answer census questions to the best of their knowledge, the Bureau learned long ago not to use legal threats to try to get people to fill out the questionnaire. That only made them suspicious and resentful. The right way was to educate them about the census, to make them understand that information collected in the census was good for the country and good for them personally.

Russell Valentine, a staff member in the Decennial Planning Division, spends his time on "outreach" programs that tell the public about the census and how census information helps everybody. "If

During the Advance Post Office Check, mail carriers make sure that every address on their route is on the master address list.

The United States Post Office delivers 98 percent of the census forms.

With field work completed, a District Office employee destroys the enumerators' kits to ensure that no one can later impersonate a census taker.

★ ★ ★ ★ ★

people don't have a basic awareness of what the census is, we're fighting a losing battle," Mr. Valentine says, and adds, "If we can get a person to pick up a pencil and start filling out the census form, he usually will finish it and send it in. The thing we have to do is get him to start."

One concern many people have is that the information they report on the census questionnaire will become public knowledge. They don't want other people to know what their income is, how much their house is worth, or how much education they have. The Census Bureau tries hard to make clear to people that the information they provide about themselves, their family, and their home is *confidential*. The Bureau is interested in that information only as a statistic, a figure to be combined with the information from millions of other census questionnaires. The picture of America emerges from all of the questionnaires together, not from the details of any one person's questionnaire.

All Census Bureau employees who work with census questionnaires must take an oath that they will treat the questionnaires as confidential. By law they can be fined or sent to prison for showing or telling the answers on a questionnaire to anyone unauthorized to have them. Not even the FBI or the Bureau of Internal Revenue can look at census questionnaires. A federal law also protects census questionnaires as confidential for seventy-two years after they are filled out.

The Census Bureau's public information program tries to spread the word everywhere about the confidentiality of the questionnaires. It also tries to explain how census information helps both government and private industry do its work better. Almost forty thousand organizations—churches, schools, the Chamber of Commerce, business and professional clubs such as Lion's and Rotary—volunteer their help in decennial census year to spread information about the value of the census.

"The Census Bureau will count heavily on the Advertising Coun-

Every Census Bureau employee, including the 300,000 temporary enumerators, must take an oath to protect the confidentiality of the information they collect.

The Census Bureau spends millions of dollars to inform the public about the census. Census Sam has appeared on TV and in newspapers.

cil for help with the 1990 census," Russell Valentine says, referring to a national organization that most newspapers, magazines, and television and radio stations belong to. "For the 1980 census we received $38 million in free advertising through the Council. Only Ford Motor Company and McDonald's spent more on advertising during that period!"

★ FOUR ★

FINDING EVERYONE

To Reach the Unreachable Goal

For Marilyn Johnson the last three days had been hard and tiring, but now she had almost finished the cleanup work for the remote area of Idaho where she was assigned as a census enumerator. Driving up narrow mountain roads that weren't easy even for her Jeep, she had stopped at each house on the route to pick up census questionnaires that had been delivered by the post office and to get questionnaires filled out at any houses the post office had missed.

At the last house listed on her address register she had asked, as she always did, whether there were any people living farther up the mountain. Yes, she was told, a miner lived "just on the other side of the mountain," three or four miles away.

Marilyn had already driven seven miles with no sign of a house; she had learned early in her census work that most people have a poor sense of distance. And as she bounced over the rocky road, she remembered the supervisor at the enumerator training program

41

telling the class that making sure everyone is counted in the rural parts of the United States is one of the hardest enumerator jobs. Marilyn definitely agreed.

Finally she spotted a ramshackle, unpainted wooden house set back from the road and turned into the rutted drive, honking to announce her arrival, as she always did. At the sound, two huge dogs bounded from under the porch and raced for her car, barking furiously. One of them put his front feet on the car and snarled at her through the window. When no one came out of the house, Marilyn tried to calm the dogs by talking to them. But the dogs weren't impressed; they weren't going to let her out of the car.

Well, Marilyn thought, *I haven't come all this way to leave without a completed census form.* She knew that if she left she would just have to come back the next day, and she certainly didn't want to do that. She settled down to wait, and so did the dogs. They fell silent but crouched beside the Jeep, their eyes fixed intently on her.

After an hour, when she was just about to give up, a truck pulled in behind her; a tall, bearded man got out and walked up to her. The dogs began barking again as if to show their master they were on the job. He silenced them with a sharp word.

"I'm from the Census Bureau," Marilyn told the man. "Is it safe for me to get out now?"

"Lady," the man said, "I wouldn't advise it."

"Did you receive a census questionnaire in the mail?" Marilyn asked.

"Don't know nothing about that," the man said.

Marilyn took a blank questionnaire from her enumerator's bag. "Well," she said firmly, "you just stand right there, and we'll fill this out together. It won't take long."

The sealskin boat finally drew in sight of Little Diomede Island, one of the most remote places in the United States, only five miles from Russia. Frank Tulik peered intently through the cold January rain that hissed as it fell into the freezing waters of the sea. Now he could

★ ★ ★ ★ ★

Enumerators travel by boat, airplane, canoe, dogsled, skis, and bicycle to get to where people are.

★ ★ ★ ★ ★

Persuading people to participate in the census sometimes means winning their confidence and trust.

The census taker is welcome in most homes in America.

just make out the houses that seemed to cling precariously to the steep slopes of the island. Frank had volunteered to take the census in this Alaskan fishing village because he could speak the local language. The last decennial census showed that only eighty people lived here. Frank wondered if even that many were still here.

In parts of Alaska the census is taken early, before the official Census Day on April 1. Although enumerators must travel by dog sled or boat to many places at that time of year, they will find most people of the villages at home, waiting for the spring thaw. After that, they will be away fishing and hunting.

As he stepped out of the boat onto the pier, Frank Tulik saw a few people standing in the doorways of their houses, watching him silently. *They think I'm crazy,* he thought. *They can't even imagine why anyone would make this trip just to fill out a piece of paper.* Tulik slipped on a patch of ice on the pier and almost fell into the sea.

"Maybe I am crazy," he said out loud.

Maria Hernandez knocked gently on the door, one of two hundred doors in the big old Brooklyn apartment building that was in her ED (enumerator district). Only sixty of the apartments had mailed back their census questionnaires. Now the hard cleanup work was beginning. Maria had been assigned to this ED because she lived in it. The Census Bureau had found that people in inner city locations and remote rural areas were more responsive to a census taker who was familiar to them.

"Mrs. Garcia, are you in there?" Maria called. "It is Maria Hernandez. I am here to take the census. We have met, Mrs. Garcia. I am Manuel Hernandez's daughter."

There was nothing but silence. Maria knew that this building had a bad reputation as a haven for drug pushers. There had been violence in the past, even shootings.

"Mrs. Garcia," Maria called again.

Now she heard locks being turned, and the door opened just the width of the chain. After a moment the chain rattled, the door swung open, and Mrs. Garcia stood there smiling.

"Oh, Maria, come in. How nice of you to come to see me. It seems I never get visitors these days, now that my children are grown. Would you like some coffee? Some cake?"

Mrs. Garcia bustled about the room, making coffee, cutting cake. "Please sit down over there, Maria, and tell me everything that is happening in your family. How is your mother? I haven't seen her in months."

Maria smiled as she sat down. It would take her an hour or more to finish, but when she left she would have the completed census questionnaire. Mrs. Hernandez trusted her; she was not a stranger.

The Enumerators

Although most census questionnaires are filled out correctly by someone in a household and mailed back to the Census Bureau, enumerators like Marilyn Johnson, Frank Tulik, and Maria Hernandez are still at the heart of every successful decennial census. Even with a successful mail out/mail back system, enumerators for the 1990 census still will have to take the census at about six million remote or hard-to-reach locations.

Enumerators also will have to follow up on an estimated thirty million homes of people who do not return their census form or who fill it out incorrectly. The Census Bureau expects to reach 106 million households in the 1990 census. That means that about one out of every three questionnaires must be attended to in some way by enumerators, and most of this work must be completed within five weeks of Census Day.

At Census Bureau headquarters in Suitland, Maryland, Stan Matchett is Associate Director for Field Operations for the 1990 decennial census. It is his job to make sure that every household in America completes a census questionnaire and to make equally sure that every person—whether in a household or not—is counted.

People live in boarded-up buildings, barns, boats, cars, and caves. The enumerator's job is to find them no matter where they are.

★　★　★　★　★

Workers in the District Offices telephone people who have filled out the forms incorrectly, to get the needed information. If they cannot reach the person by phone, an enumerator makes a home visit.

Matchett knows perhaps better than anyone the importance of enumerators to the success of the census, and he recently talked about that.

"We really try to find everyone and collect the best information we can about everyone," he said. "The credibility of the census and the Census Bureau depends on people believing we go all out to make a complete count.

"Enumerators are crucial to that. The work will be harder for them in the 1990 census than it was in 1980. In 1980, 85 percent of the households mailed back their questionnaires. The Census Bureau doesn't expect more than a 70 percent mail back in 1990, and that will mean more work and harder work for the enumerators."

Then Matchett talked about why such a big drop in household mail back of questionnaires is expected. "Ten years is a long time," he said, referring to the decade between the 1980 and 1990 censuses. "Society changes. There are a lot more illegal aliens in the country now, and most of them don't want to fill out a census. Inner city slums have grown.

"People are bombarded with junk mail now. They throw it away without looking at it, and sometimes census questionnaires get thrown out with it. People are on the move more than ever. People on the move are hard to count. All this makes the enumerator's job harder."

The Census Bureau will need approximately three hundred thousand enumerators for the 1990 decennial census. Such a huge number is needed because it takes time to follow up on the expected thirty million people who won't return their questionnaires or who will fill them out incorrectly. Another reason for the large work force is that the information must be gathered so quickly. Most enumerators will be on the job only four to six weeks.

Who are the enumerators, these people who work for the Census Bureau for just a few weeks every ten years and yet are so important to the decennial census's success? Over the years, more and more women have become enumerators; since World War II they have

49

made up 90 percent of the enumerator work force. There are several reasons for this. One is that women have a better chance of getting into a house to conduct an interview or go over an incorrectly filled-out questionnaire. Many people will refuse to let a strange man into the house, even though he has papers showing he is from the Census Bureau.

Women make good enumerators because they tend to have more patience than men in puzzling over faulty questionnaires and because they are persistent in telephone calls and visits until they have found someone who has not turned in his questionnaire. Also, in the past women have been freer than men to take short-term work. But that has changed in the past ten years as increasing millions of women have entered the full-time job market.

All kinds of people apply to become enumerators. Some are unemployed; some are retired; others want only occasional work. The Census Bureau is now more flexible about hiring people with full-time jobs who want to work part time as enumerators. The Bureau also makes a special effort to recruit people who speak Spanish, Vietnamese, and other languages now widely spoken in America. But one thing is certain: a high percentage of enumerators for the 1990 census still will be women.

Sometimes the work of enumerators is boring as they pour over incorrectly filled out questionnaires and try to reach people by telephone to clarify answers. Sometimes it is frustrating as they go back to a house time after time to try to find someone at home. On T-night (T stands for transients or people on the move), enumerators visit camp grounds, bus and train stations, motels, and YMCAs and YWCAs to count those who may have been missed when questionnaires were mailed. And few enumerators like "casual count" night—sometimes called S-night (shelter night)—when enumerators must go out onto city streets to count the homeless. Then they comb the slums, parks, overnight shelters, welfare offices, and food lines. They get as much information as possible from the homeless, but

Even people in jails or prisons are counted in the Census.

College students are counted in the states where they attend school. Here census forms are placed in dormitory mailboxes.

During the "casual count" enumerators go to parks, pool halls, welfare offices, and street corners to find people who have no fixed address.

sometimes that is no more than writing down what they can see: such things as sex, approximate age, and race.

Sometimes enumerators are called on to make an unusual effort. In a New York field office during the 1980 census, all completed questionnaires were destroyed in a fire. The enumerators had to take the census again as fast as possible in a difficult part of New York City. Also in 1980, one month after Census Day when the follow-up work was in full swing, the Mount Saint Helens volcano in Washington state exploded, spewing millions of tons of ash into the sky. Dozens of towns were evacuated and their occupants taken to emergency shelters just at a time census workers were confirming vacant houses and trying to find people who had not returned their questionnaires.

"But work had to continue," recalls Rick Schweitzer, Regional Director for Field Operations in the area at the time. "In some places the dust was so thick you couldn't see. In Yakima the office had to close for a week because of the dust. Work was delayed over a month, but we got it done. We found everyone."

Enumerators receive about $5.50 an hour, hardly a high wage for the work they do. Recruiting would seem to be a great problem, and sometimes it is. The Census Bureau must have enumerators who take the work seriously, will not get discouraged, and understand the importance of what they are doing.

Fortunately, over the years the Census Bureau has built up a recruiting network; and as it gears up for the decennial census, 450 district recruiting offices are opened all over the country. Stan Matchett estimates that two million applicants will be tested as enumerators for the 1990 census and that six hundred thousand of them will be put into training. Training consists of three days of learning the questionnaires, doing mock interviews, and learning to use and fill out census maps. The training staff studies the trainees closely and narrows the group down to the three hundred thousand who will finally be chosen as field enumerators.

But the selection doesn't end there. Enumerators are assigned to the field in teams of eight, and the team is headed by an experienced supervisor. The supervisor watches the work of the team closely. If someone can't handle the interviewing or is lazy or careless, he or she will be fired immediately and replaced by a reserve enumerator. The pressure to get the work done, to meet the deadline, is too great to try to improve a poor worker.

Jerry Potosky was an enumerator crew leader for the 1970 decennial census and has worked on special Census Bureau surveys for years. She knows very well how hard the work is. "Lots of people won't open their door," she says, "and it's impossible to convince some people that you're not going to use the information to make trouble for them. You never know when you knock on a door what you're going to run into.

"The cleanup work of the census is the hardest. These are the people who haven't returned their questionnaire by mail and haven't responded to the telephone follow-up. Only the very dedicated enumerators are usually left at this point. Getting the questionnaire completed might mean traveling for miles out into isolated country. It might mean visiting an inner city apartment several times. We count on good relationships with apartment building managers in the ghetto areas. If we can't get the people to respond, the managers can help with information like the number of people in the household and their approximate ages.

"Some places have Complete Count Committees. These are committees of local politicians and business people who help get word out about the census and ease the way for census workers. They know it's in the best interest of their community to have a complete count."

Why do some enumerators stay on the job until everything that can be done to make the census count complete has been done?

"Dedication," says Jerry Potosky. "We are determined that the statistics we collect are going to reflect our area the way it is. We have the satisfaction of a job well done. But we're usually glad when it's over."

In rural areas many census workers work from home offices. A crew leader in Maine coordinates the work of census takers from her dining-room office.

Enumerators have a lot to learn in the three-day training sessions.

In rural areas, mobile census units are sometimes used where people can come to get help with filling out their forms.

The enumerators must follow up on the 30 million forms that are not mailed back or that are filled out incorrectly.

Hard as it is, the enumerator's job has its rewards and excitements. Over the years enumerators have helped kids with their homework, sat down to dinner with families they came to interview, and had cheering conversations with thousands of lonely people. Occasionally enumerators have arrived just in time to help in an emergency—delivering a baby or calling an ambulance for an injured or sick person. They travel in kayaks and airplanes, in sleds and on horseback, by bicycle and bus to cover their districts. The job of finding everyone depends on them, and they know it.

★ FIVE ★

SPECIAL CENSUS COUNT PROBLEMS

Undercount: The Invisible People

IN the end the goal of finding everyone is unreachable. "Some people don't want to be found," says Stan Matchett. "Some people just don't care."

The Census Bureau knows that it misses people in the decennial census count because it does surveys after the census to check on how accurate its work has been. The regional offices hire completely new teams of enumerators and send them to carefully selected sample areas to make sure each household has been included in the census.

The undercount—as people missed are called—is small; in the 1980 census the undercount was estimated to be 1.4 percent. But a 1.4 percent undercount means that over three million people in the

United States were missed in the census count. That is equivalent to missing the whole state of Iowa.

The people they miss are out there. The Census Bureau knows that. But they seem to be invisible, and that worries and embarrasses the Bureau.

The greatest worry is that the undercount is higher for certain groups than for others. It is higher in cities than in rural and suburban areas and higher in the South than in other parts of the country. More men than women are missed, more blacks than whites, more poor than rich, more young than old. More young black men are not counted than any other group. An estimated 5.9 percent were not counted in the 1980 census.

The problem is clear and serious: some of the people most important to count are not being counted. State and city governments receive federal money for welfare and public health services, job training, and education programs based on the number of people who need help of these kinds. If these people are missed in the census count, the city and state governments where they live will receive less federal money to help them.

What can be done about this problem? Cities with large numbers of poor people and young blacks and Hispanics want the census count adjusted upward. They argue that since the Census Bureau knows there is an undercount and approximately how much it is, they should receive money based on that knowledge. The Bureau's estimate is that the undercount in the 1990 census will be between 1 and 2 percent, but the Department of Commerce has made a decision that there will be no undercount adjustment in the 1990 census.

Department of Commerce officials point out that the Constitution calls for an actual count of people in the census. The Census Bureau also is concerned that if the government begins changing the census count—even in an effort to make it more accurate—people may be suspicious. People might also feel that it is not so important to be counted since the count may be changed anyway.

Should Illegal Aliens Be Counted in the Census?

The Constitution requires that every person who lives in the United States be counted in the census, but should the census include people who are living in this country illegally? Our political representation in Congress is based on population counts in the various states. Because there are an estimated three to six million people living in the United States who entered the country illegally, the counting of illegal aliens has become a hotly debated issue.

As amended by section 2 of the Fourteenth Amendment, the Constitution reads, "Representatives shall be apportioned among the states according to their respective numbers, counting whole numbers of persons in each state. . . ." The Constitution does not refer to citizens or legal residents but rather to "persons."

The Census Bureau has always interpreted the Constitution to mean that everyone living in the United States should be counted. Thus, U. S. military personnel and U. S. diplomats stationed in foreign countries are not counted in the census. Citizens of foreign countries living in the United States are counted, regardless of whether they are here legally or illegally.

The problem arises because there are only 435 representatives allowed by law in Congress's House of Representatives. Each of the fifty states is given one representative regardless of its population. The remaining 385 representatives are divided among the states according to their populations as they are reported after every decennial census.

This means that if a state has a large number of illegal aliens in its population, it may gain a representative at the expense of a state whose population does not contain many illegals. California and New York are states with large numbers of illegal aliens. The Census Bureau estimates that after the 1980 census each of these states would have had one seat less in Congress had it not been for their large illegal alien populations. On the other hand, Indiana, which does not have many illegals, lost a seat. If illegal aliens are included

61

Census workers review completed census forms in a District Office.

★ ★ ★ ★ ★

Census questionnaires are available in both Spanish and English.

in the 1990 census, Pennsylvania and Connecticut may lose Congressional representatives.

Some states are understandably concerned and have proposed laws that would keep people who are in this country illegally from being counted in census totals that are used for determining the number of representatives to Congress. Congressman Hal Daub of Nebraska, testifying before the House Subcommittee on Census and Population, expressed the feeling of many when he said, "In my estimation, the prospect of Nebraskans at some future point effectively losing representation in Congress to illegal, undocumented, non-voting, law-breaking aliens is simply outrageous."

Those who oppose the inclusion of illegal aliens in the census count point out that at the time the Constitution was written there was no such thing as an illegal alien. Anyone who could get passage to this new country was free to enter and live here. It was not until the late 1800s that Congress passed the first law restricting the entry of foreigners. The Founding Fathers did not foresee a time when free entry to the United States would be limited; they could not have foreseen a time when there would be three to six million people living in the country illegally—a number as large as the entire U. S. population at the time of the first census. Therefore, in writing the Constitution, they did not consider illegal entry.

At present there is no question on the census form that asks whether a person is a legal resident of the United States. Even if there were such a question, it is doubtful that a person would admit to being here illegally; quite possibly the illegal would not fill out the questionnaire. But for many reasons we need to know how many people are in the country and where they are, regardless of whether they are here legally or illegally.

The problem is a serious and perplexing one, but the Census Bureau plans to continue to count everyone, as the Constitution directs.

★ SIX ★

PROCESSING CENSUS RESULTS

Automation

Wʜᴇɴ the awesome task of collecting 106 million questionnaires for the 1990 census has been completed, another task of gigantic proportions will begin. Each questionnaire contains dozens of pieces of information about every person and household in America; the long form may contain hundreds. This information is of no value until it is taken from the questionnaires, compiled, and combined into statistics that tell us the thousands of things that make up the picture of America.

How many children will enter first grade in 1993? What is the average income of Hispanics in Los Angeles? How great is the need for low-cost housing in Philadelphia? Will increased migration to Arizona and Florida cause serious highway problems and water shortages? How many households now have only one parent? Answers to questions like these are but a tiny fraction of the information that will come from the statistics based on the 1990 census.

The Hollerith Electric Tabulating Machine, first used in the 1890 census, was the forerunner of the modern computer. It enabled census data to be processed faster and more accurately.

In 1990 the machines for taking information from the census questionnaires will be more highly developed than ever before. This use of sophisticated machines, called automation, means that the data will be more accurate than in the past and that the results will be tabulated faster. With twenty-five million more people to count and 20 percent more households in 1990 than in 1980, the need for increased and improved automation is great.

The Census Bureau: An Automation Pioneer

Because of the massive amounts of information that make up the census, the Census Bureau has always been a leader in developing new data processing techniques. In 1889 Herman Hollerith, a Census Bureau employee, developed the Hollerith Electric Tabulating Machine; this machine recorded information using holes punched in cards and then tabulated the results. The new machine was used in the 1890 census. Later Hollerith started a company based on his invention; in time, the company became International Business Machines (IBM).

In the 1940s, the Bureau sponsored the development of UNIVAC-I, the first main-frame computer designed to process massive amounts of data. But the data still had to be keyed in by keypunch operators, which slowed down the process a great deal. So the Bureau developed FOSDIC (Film Optical Sensing Device for Input to Computers), which can read filled-in dots on the forms and translate the information so that it can be processed by computer.

FOSDIC is still used as the basis for the FACT-90 system that will process the questionnaires for the 1990 census. FACT stands for FOSDIC and Automated Camera Technology. The system consists of high-speed cameras that film the questionnaires, a unit to process the microfilm, and FOSDIC, which transfers the data from the film onto computer readable tape.

Processing census data cards in the 1940s.

This pantograph punch was used to process the 1890 and 1900 censuses.

Tabulating census results in the 1920s.

Tabulating census results in the 1930s.

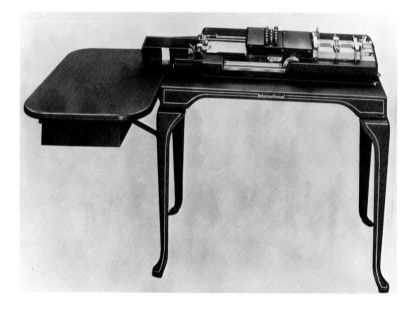

Punch card machine used in the 1930s.

*FOSDIC reads filled-in dots on the census forms and translates them
into computer readable form so that the data can be tabulated. The
address of a household and the name of the respondent cannot be read
by FOSDIC, so it is at this point that an individual's name and the rest
of the information are separated, thus ensuring confidentiality.*

★ ★ ★ ★ ★

In 1990 the completed questionnaires will be processed through FACT-90. The computer will perform some edits automatically. For example, if a six-year-old child is indicated to be a schoolteacher, the computer will correct this obvious error. If the form is incomplete it will be rejected and sent to an enumerator for follow-up by telephone interview or a visit to the household that sent in the faulty questionnaire.

One of the biggest jobs is coding answers on the response forms. While many questions are multiple choice and can be answered by filling in a dot that can be read by FOSDIC, other questions, such as language spoken or occupation, call for a variety of written answers, and the responses must be coded before the computer can tabulate them. In previous censuses, hundreds of coding clerks were employed to look up the codes and write them on the forms. Many errors were made. In 1990 the clerk will type the answer into the computer, and the computer will assign the proper code. This will be much faster and more accurate and will save the Census Bureau $25 million.

Census Geography

In order for most of the information collected in the census to be useful, it has to be associated with a geographic area. The most obvious example is that of deciding the number of representatives for Congress. The population of the country must be broken down by states in order to determine the number of representatives each state is entitled to in the House of Representatives. States must know the population of counties to be able to determine voting districts. Business and industry need information about people who live in specific areas—income, ages, education, race or nationality—in order to make decisions about investing money in new businesses or factories. City planners need to know not only the number of children in a city but where in the city they live in order to build schools and day care facilities in the right places.

Automated bar-code scanners record the receipt of the census forms when they are mailed back to the district offices.

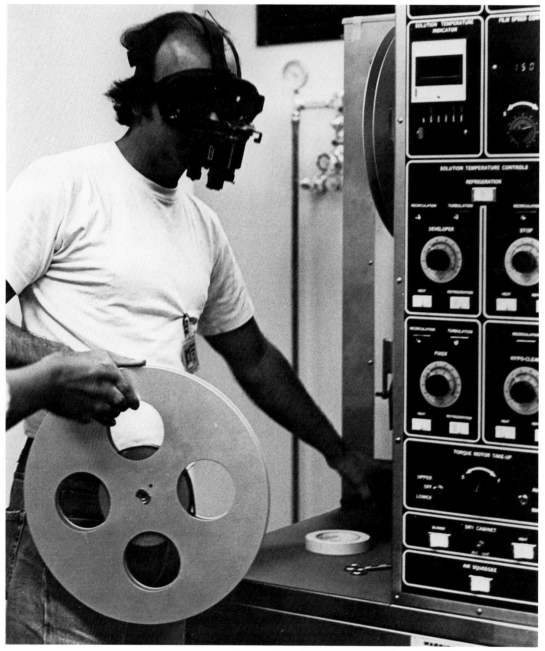

A microfilm technician inspects part of the 6,000 miles of microfilm used to record information from the 1980 census. Microfilm combined with an optical and electronic scanning system makes it possible for the Census Bureau to tabulate information 1.5 million times faster than the clerks who processed the first census in 1790.

The Census Bureau reports information using two kinds of boundaries—governmental and economic. Areas defined by their governmental boundaries are the familiar ones of state, county, city, voting district, and township. Economic units are called metropolitan statistical areas (MSAs). These are geographic areas that function as a unit economically regardless of their governmental boundaries.

An MSA might contain two cities and surrounding suburbs like Minneapolis–Saint Paul. It might be made up of parts of a larger number of governmental areas. For example, the Washington, D. C., metropolitan area contains a large city and surrounding suburbs that are in two states, three counties, and the independent city of Alexandria. A person might live in Montgomery County in Maryland, work in Washington, and go out to eat in Alexandria, which is in Virginia.

When several governmental units are united so closely as an economic area, it is important to have data about that area as a whole. The Census Bureau has defined 282 such metropolitan statistical areas throughout the United States. More than three-fourths of the nation's population live in these urban centers.

In order that census information can be most effectively used, it often must be assigned to both a geographical area and an economic area. In past censuses this has been a gigantic manual task. For the 1980 census, 1,200 Census Bureau mapmakers produced 300,000 hand-drawn maps that covered every area in the United States. They had to write in 63,000 names of each area, 45,000 census tract numbers, and 2,500,000 block numbers. Every house had to be assigned to a block. Each block was included in every political unit to which it belonged and, if appropriate, included in a metropolitan statistical area. Many errors were made in this process, and often the maps and lists were incorrect.

TIGER to the Rescue

The Census Bureau had so many problems with mapmaking in 1980 that in 1981 it began developing a new system. That system is called TIGER, and it is the most exciting innovation in automation that the

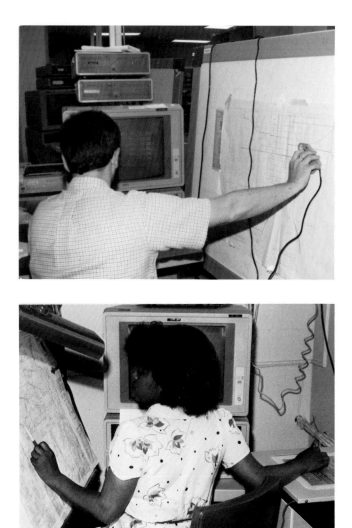

Inputting information from old maps into the computer to build the Census Bureau's automated map system, TIGER.

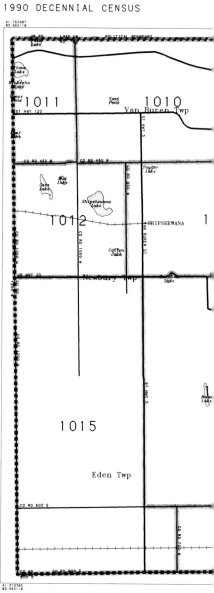

BUREAU OF THE CENSUS
U.S. DEPARTMENT OF COMMERCE
BASE MAP GENERATED USING DIGITAL DATA OBTAINED
AT 1:100,000-SCALE THROUGH A COOPERATIVE PROGRAM
WITH THE UNITED STATES GEOLOGICAL SURVEY
DEPARTMENT OF THE INTERIOR.

MAP GENERATED: 02/27/88

COUNTY LOCATOR MAP

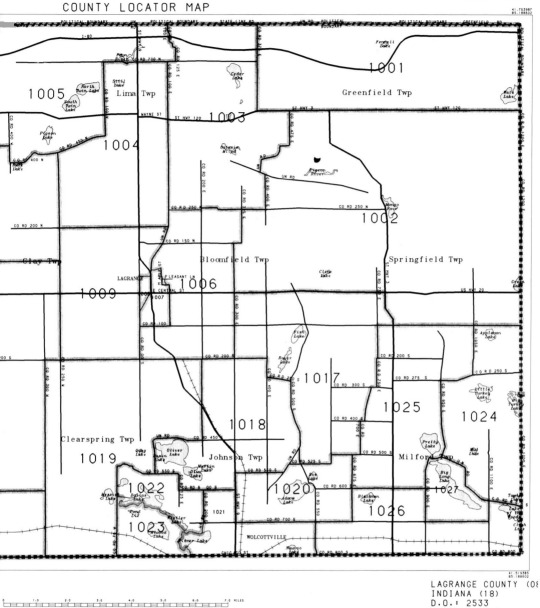

LAGRANGE COUNTY (08
INDIANA (18)
D.O.: 2533
SHEET 1 OF 1

This map of LaGrange County, Indiana, was produced by a computer system called TIGER, which stands for Topographically Integrated Geographical Encoding and Referencing. TIGER is one of the largest computer files in the world. The map will be used by enumerators to indicate where houses not already included on the master address list are located.

Bureau will use in the 1990 census. TIGER stands for Topographically Integrated Geographical Encoding and Referencing; it is one of the largest computer files in the world with fifty billion bytes (characters) of information in its vast memory. With TIGER the three geographical tools necessary to the census—maps, every business and household address, and the names and boundaries of all geographical areas such as counties and voting districts—are brought together in one computer system.

TIGER can produce maps of the entire United States. These maps, drawn on a scale of 1:100,000, show every city and town, street, road, railroad, airport, and body of water. During the 1990 precensus all features on the maps were verified by enumerators as they checked for any addresses missing from their address lists. In this way the maps will be updated before each census in the future. The three hundred thousand maps needed for the 1990 census—one for each enumerator area—were produced by TIGER.

A computer file that has the entire United States in its memory has many uses. A few examples: Emergency personnel can key in an address, and the quickest route to the scene of an emergency will appear on a computer screen in an ambulance or fire truck. Taxi fleets, couriers, and trucking companies can use this file in the same way, improving performance and profits. A product called The Navigator that displays a map on a computer screen for use in cars is now available. Since each housing unit is assigned to a geographical location in the TIGER system, the government could determine instantly the value of all property destroyed in a hurricane or other natural disaster.

Advances in computer technology doubtless will continue. Bob LaMacchia, Assistant Division Chief for Planning for the Geography Division, is a man who has seen the awesome development in census automation and knows it will continue. But he also knows that a good census will continue to depend on human beings.

"No matter how automated the census gets," he says, "enumerators will always have to go out and find people."

★ SEVEN ★

HOW AMERICA USES CENSUS INFORMATION

THE great task of collecting information from tens of millions of households is finished. The equally huge task of taking the information from the questionnaires and processing it through the Census Bureau's complex machines has been completed. The Bureau's computers have billions of pieces of information stored in their almost limitless memory.

Now begins the work of taking the tabulated figures, analyzing them, and reporting them in a way that they can be understood and used by the nation. Scores of reports and studies will be issued with such titles as "Ancestry of the Population by State," "Women in the American Economy," and "County Business Patterns." Private research institutions using the new Census Bureau data will publish hundreds of studies.

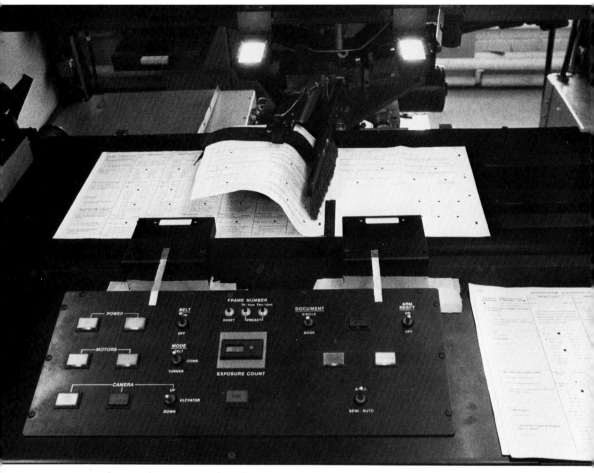

High-speed cameras film the questionnaires as the brush turns the pages.

The Way We Are

From these studies and reports will emerge a picture of America as it looked on Census Day in the year the census was taken. This picture can be compared with the one developed from the previous census and ones before that. The great value of these pictures is that they tell us how we have changed, how we look now, and where we may be heading in the future. With these pictures, with the knowledge they give us, we have our best chance of making decisions that are the right ones for our country and, sometimes, for ourselves as individuals.

Here is just a small part of the picture of America as it was revealed by the 1980 census:

—Our national population grew from 203,302,031 in 1970 to 226,545,805 in 1980. So we are still growing, but the rate of growth is slowing down. It was just 11.4 percent in this ten-year period, the slowest decennial growth in this century. Census projections are that the slowdown will continue into the next century.

—Females outnumber males in our country, but not by much. The female count was 116,492,644, the male count 110,053,161. Females were 51.4 percent of our population, which was almost the same as the 1970 figure of 51.3.

—Some racial and ethnic groups grew much faster than others during the ten years between the 1970 and 1980 censuses. For example, the black population increased by 17.3 percent, but people of Spanish origin in the United States increased by 61 percent and people of Asian origin by 127.5 percent! This large increase by Hispanics and Asians resulted mostly from immigration.

—The American family continues to change. The census of 1800 showed an average family size of seven children. Because of urbanization, industrialization, and other economic factors, family size has declined steadily since 1800 (except for a brief "baby boom" in the twenty years following World War II). The average completed family size in 1980 was (or was expected to be) about two children. Other

81

1990
Census of the
United States

A message from
the Director
Bureau of the Census

We are conducting the 21st decennial census of our Nation. Starting in 1790, when Thomas Jefferson directed the first decennial census, the census has monitored the vital signs of our great country. To preserve this legacy, I hope that we can count on you to participate by completing this form.

You may ask, "Why should I count myself in the census?" Although a law requires that you respond to the census, I hope that you choose to respond knowing that the results of the census are used to ensure fair representation in our government and to improve the quality of your life. For the sake of our Nation and your community, take this opportunity to put yourself in the picture by responding to the Bicentennial Census.

Perhaps you may be concerned that by participating, your name and information soon will be available to others. That is not the case. Federal law protects the confidentiality of your responses for the next 72 years, or until April 1, 2062. Until then, no one sees your completed form except Census Bureau workers, who are sworn to hold it in confidence and can be fined and/or imprisoned for disclosing information.

The census is vitally important, so stand right up for who you are. You do so by filling out this form accurately and completely. Kindly **return it by Census Day, April 1, 1990,** or as close to that date as possible. PLEASE DO MAIL IT BACK in the envelope provided. Doing so will save the expense and inconvenience of a personal visit from a census taker.

Your answers are confidential

By law (Title 13, U.S. Code), census employees are subject to fine and/or imprisonment for any disclosure of your answers. Only after 72 years can your individual census form become available to other government agencies or the public. The same law requires that you answer the questions to the best of your knowledge.

Para personas de habla hispana

(For Spanish-speaking persons): SI USTED DESEA UN CUESTIONARIO DEL CENSO EN ESPAÑOL llame a la oficina del censo. El número de teléfono se encuentra en el encasillado de la dirección.

A message from the Director of the Bureau of the Census, John Keane, stresses the importance of filling out the form and the confidentiality of the information.

important changes in the family revealed by the 1980 census: Median age at first marriage is 25.9 years for men, 23.6 years for women—up more than two years for both sexes since 1970. This could provide a greater chance for family stability, since young marriages have a higher risk of failure. The divorce rate has stabilized since 1960; even so, at the current rate, 50 percent of all recent marriages will end in divorce. Nineteen percent of all households with minor children are headed by a woman with no husband present. Almost 50 percent of married mothers of preschool children now hold a paid job outside the home.

—Although our national growth rate is slowing down, there are many more households than ever before, a rise from 63.4 million in 1970 to 80.4 million in 1980. One reason for this was that the large number of baby boomers were now old enough to start their own families. Another major reason is that—as noted above—more people are staying single longer now or deciding not to get married at all, greatly increasing the number of one-member households. The result is a great need for more houses and apartments.

—We are growing older as a nation. The number of persons under eighteen decreased by 8.5 percent between 1970 and 1980. The number of persons sixty-five and older increased by 27.9 percent. Changes like these will have a major impact on American society and economy in the future.

—The 1980 census showed that, for the first time in our nation's history, at least half the residents over age twenty-five in every state had completed high school.

—For the first time more than half of working-age women (age sixteen and older) were in the job market—52 percent compared to 43 percent in 1970.

—While incomes doubled between 1970 and 1980, the buying power of incomes rose just 5 percent. This was because of the rising cost of living. By comparison, between the 1960 and 1970 censuses, buying power rose 35 percent.

—The number of poor people stayed about the same between

1970 and 1980, but poverty among families headed by a woman with no husband rose sharply.

—Ninety percent of the nation's population growth in the past decade was in the South and West. For the first time, more than half of the country's people (52.3 percent) are living in those two regions.

—Americans are a very mobile society. The census showed that nearly half of our population was living in a different house or apartment in 1980 than in 1970.

How Government Uses the Census

After each census the President of the United States reports to Congress the new population figures for each state; the number of members of the House of Representatives for each state will be based on these figures. The Reapportionment Act of 1929 fixed the number of representatives to the House at 435; the purpose of this 435 limit was to keep this body of Congress from becoming too large as the country's population grew. Therefore, there is now a reshuffling of seats in the House of Representatives as our national population grows and shifts.

The reapportionment is based on a complex mathematical formula that gives each state one representative and then divides the remaining 385 seats among the states according to the relative sizes of their populations. The allotment of representatives is also based on the concept of equal representation—that each person's vote is worth the same as every other person's. Therefore, each state is divided into voting districts: one district for each representative to be elected.

These districts must be of approximately equal population if each representative is to represent the same number of people in Congress. Therefore after each census the states must redraw their voting district boundaries (redistricting) based on the new population figures. They must also adjust the number of districts according to whether the state has lost or gained one or more representatives.

Based on the 1980 census count, states that lost population or grew slowly lost seats in the House of Representatives to faster-growing states. Here is what happened:

States that Lost

New York—5 seats
Illinois, Ohio, Pennsylvania—2 seats
Indiana, Massachusetts, Michigan, Missouri, New Jersey,
    South Dakota—1 seat

States that Gained

Florida—4 seats
Texas—3 seats
California—2 seats
Arizona, Colorado, Nevada, New Mexico, Oregon, Tennessee,
    Utah, Washington—1 seat

Another important use of census information is in determining how huge amounts of federal tax dollars will be distributed to state and local governments for a wide variety of programs. More than a hundred of these programs are concerned with improving the quality of people's lives: low-cost housing, job training, adult education, highway expansion and improvement, slum clearance and urban renewal, to name but a few. To distribute this money fairly—more than $50 billion annually—it is necessary to pinpoint the areas of greatest need.

Where in the country are the concentrations of poor housing? Where are the areas of greatest unemployment and lowest income? Where are people lagging behind in schooling? Where are they having the hardest time getting to work and how do they get to their jobs? Information gathered in the decennial census can answer all these questions and hundreds of others that are necessary to make wise decisions about sharing federal money for the public good. In fact, only the census can answer most of them in a clear and impartial way.

The census helps local governments in planning for the future. All across America city and county governments are using census figures to study population growth and project future trends. These studies will determine where schools, fire stations, police stations, hospitals, water and sewage plants will be built in the years ahead. Such structures are expensive; they must serve a useful purpose for twenty-five years or more to pay for themselves. Census population statistics take much of the guesswork out of planning for the future.

How Business and Industry Use the Census

A health care association on the West Coast is searching for the best locations to start several new medical clinics. It uses census data to find communities with high numbers of recently married couples with young children. A chain of toy stores does exactly the same thing.

A new magazine appealing to Spanish-speaking Americans plans its advertising campaign on the basis of census statistics showing parts of the country with large Hispanic populations with incomes and education levels that might make them interested in such a magazine.

A company that manufactures plastic containers plans to build a new factory. Many workers will be needed, and the company cannot pay high salaries. Company officials study census figures to find places in the country where unemployment is high and where the cost of living is relatively low.

The 1960 census revealed a large and growing group of men and women in the eighteen to twenty-four age range. The Ford Motor Company wanted to develop a car that would appeal to that very active car-buying group. The result was the hugely successful Mustang, introduced in 1964.

Boxed census questionnaires arrive at a processing center to be microfilmed.

As these examples show, American industry and business have discovered how to use the census. Census figures on population, age patterns, sex, education, income, and other characteristics of the American people have become indispensable planning tools for corporations and businesses. They use census information in deciding how much demand there is likely to be for a new product. They use it to choose communities where their products are most likely to be bought.

When you go to a McDonald's for a Big Mac or to Wendy's for a hamburger or when your mother stops at a Seven Eleven for a carton of milk she forgot to get at the supermarket, you can be sure that census information was used in deciding where to build those places. "Profiles" on almost seventy thousand communities and political and economic subdivisions of the United States can be drawn from census data. These profiles will include the number of people, the number of families, the ages of the children, the number of cars, family incomes, and other information important to fast food chains and convenience stores. The census data will even reveal traffic patterns.

"For the Seven Elevens and Roy Rogers of this world, location is everything," says Stephen Tordella of the Population Reference Bureau. "It isn't enough to be located at the right intersection. You have to be on the right corner of the right intersection."

If you are a businessman, census data can help put you there.

★ EIGHT ★

FACTFINDER FOR THE NATION

THE work of the Census Bureau never ends. America wants and needs information about itself. It needs to know how one section of the country is progressing compared to others. It needs to know about economic, educational, and other differences between the many racial and ethnic groups that make up America. It needs to know about salary differences between men and women in business and industry. The country must know what is happening in its basic industries such as agriculture, mining, and manufacturing and in its retail and wholesale trade.

The Census Bureau is by no means the only organization that collects information about what is happening in America. Almost every other part of government, such as the Department of Transportation and the Department of Housing and Urban Development, gathers data important to its work. American universities and private industry carry out vast amounts of research.

The nation's transportation networks, which move people and merchandise from one place to another, are very important to the economy. The Census of Transportation is conducted every five years and provides information on the volume of personal travel, truck inventory, and transportation energy use. These data are used with information from the decennial census on place of work, car pooling, and public transportation use.

But compared to the Census Bureau, all other social science research organizations are small. The Bureau has almost nine thousand full-time professional employees. Statisticians make up the largest group, but there are many demographers (population specialists), economists, geographers, cartographers (mapmakers), and computer experts on the staff. This professional staff is strategically placed all over the United States. In addition to its headquarters in the massive old yellow-brick building near Washington, D. C., the Bureau has regional offices in Atlanta, Boston, Chicago, Dallas, Denver, Detroit, Los Angeles, New York City, Philadelphia, Seattle, Charlotte, North Carolina, and Kansas City, Kansas.

For all its size, for all its staff and offices, the Census Bureau is no bigger than the work for which it is responsible. A nation that changes as fast as the United States cannot wait a decade for current, up-to-the-minute information. The ten-year gap between the decennial censuses is too long. The great data bases provided by these censuses must be supplemented and updated constantly. That is the unending task that Congress has given to the Census Bureau.

The Bureau began fifty years ago to meet the continuous information needs of government, industry, and the general public by conducting what it calls the Current Population Survey. In this survey about sixty thousand households are interviewed every month on many subjects to keep decennial census figures updated on family size and composition, income, employment, birth rates, migration, and a number of other topics. This current information, added to the decennial census, helps to guide government, educational, and business planners in making decisions crucial to America's future.

Every five years the Census Bureau takes a census of our country's major industries—agriculture, construction, mining and oil production—so that government and the private sector will have a clearer idea of what is happening in those critical areas of America's economy. In addition, the Bureau conducts regular surveys of health, crime, food prices, and other subjects of special concern to the American people.

Having up-to-date information is so important that Congress has authorized the Census Bureau to conduct a mid-decade census. The first mid-decade census may be held in 1995. It will not be of the scope of the decennial census, and the results will not be used to determine seats in Congress; but the results obtained from extensive sampling will provide current information that will be useful in many ways.

Two hundred years of asking questions, recording answers, and processing and analyzing information have given the Census Bureau unmatched experience. Congress, other government agencies, and the private sector acknowledge the Bureau's skill and trustworthiness. Most people are willing to give it accurate and confidential information.

With considerable pride, the Census Bureau calls itself Factfinder for the Nation.

GLOSSARY OF CENSUS TERMS

Apportionment. The means by which each state is assured equal representation in the House of Representatives. The size of this branch of Congress is limited by the Reapportionment Act of 1929 to 435 members. Each of the fifty states is given one representative regardless of its population. The remaining 385 representatives are divided proportionally among the states according to the size of their populations. A difference of only a few thousand people could mean losing or gaining a representative. This makes an accurate census count of crucial importance.

Baby Boom. The dramatic increase in the number of children born in the United States following World War II, between 1946 and 1964. In the past twenty years the "baby boomers" have begun families of their own, and this has led to an increase in the need for schools, day care centers, and health programs for children.

Census Day. April 1 of every year that ends in zero. Since 1930, the decennial census has counted everyone who is living in the United States on that day. Thus, a baby born on April 2, 1990, will not be counted until the census is taken in the year 2000.

Census Tracts. Subdivisions of counties into units that contain an average of four thousand people. The Census Bureau gathers statistics for census tracts so that changes in the population and economy of these small areas can be followed over time.

Demography. The science that describes the vital statistics of a population (such as age, birth and death rates, sex) and population distribution in certain geographical areas.

Emigrant. A person who leaves one country to live permanently in another.

Enumerator. A person employed by the Census Bureau, usually on a temporary basis, to take the census: find people, count them, interview them, and help them fill out census questionnaires.

Gerrymander. To divide a voting area so that one political party has a majority in as many districts as possible, giving it an unfair advantage in an election.

Hispanics. People who can trace their ancestry to Spanish-speaking countries.

Immigrant. A person who enters a country from another with the intention of settling there.

Mail Out/Mail Back System. The collection of census data by mailing questionnaires to households and asking that the completed questionnaires be mailed back to the Census Bureau.

MSA. Metropolitan Statistical Area: a large city with surrounding suburbs that functions as a social and economic unit. It may be made up of several political units: counties, towns, etc.

Outreach. A publicity effort aimed at encouraging those people most likely to be left out of the census to participate. Outreach uses mass media advertising and encourages communities to start "complete count" committees to encourage participation in the census and thus minimize the undercount.

Population. The total number of people in a country, state, or other area or place.

Precanvass. To update and correct the Census Bureau's master address list prior to mailing out the census questionnaire.

Sampling. Selecting a small segment of a population to represent the whole group. The 17 percent of households that will receive the long form of the 1990 census questionnaire will be a sample population of the entire country.

Self-enumeration. The process by which a householder fills out a census questionnaire himself or herself instead of answering the questions for a census enumerator.

S-Night. Street and Shelter Night. On this night, enumerators try to find and count vagrants and homeless people in the cities.

Statistics. The science of classifying, tabulating, and analyzing facts in a numerical way. When we say that a population is 52 percent female and 48 percent male or 60 percent white, 25 percent black, and 15 percent Asian, we are describing the population statistically.

Survey. A statistical examination by the Census Bureau of areas of national concern such as housing, employment, crime, health, and business activity. Usually these surveys are conducted on a regular basis.

T-Night A night soon after Census Day when enumerators visit hotels, YWCAs, train stations, and camp grounds to find people in transit who might have been missed by the Census.

Undercount. The number of those people who are not found and therefore not counted in the census.

BIBLIOGRAPHY

Bounpane, Peter A. "The Census Looks to 1990." *American Demographics,* Oct. 1983.

——. "Looking Toward 1990: Planning the Next United States Census of Population and Housing." *Government Publications Review,* Vol. 12, 1985.

A Century of Population Growth: From the First Census of the United States to the Twelfth, 1790–1900. Washington, D. C., Government Printing Office, 1907.

Francese, Peter K. "The 1980 Census: The Counting of America." *Population Bulletin,* Vol. 34, No. 4, Sept. 1979 (Population Reference Bureau, Washington, D. C.).

Kaplan, Charles P., and Thomas Van Valey and Associates. *Census '80: Continuing the Factfinder Tradition.* Washington, D. C.: U. S. Bureau of the Census, 1980.

Merrick, Thomas W., and Stephen J. Tordella. "Demographics: People and Markets." *Population Bulletin,* Vol. 43, No. 1, Feb. 1988 (Population Reference Bureau, Washington, D. C.).

Riley, David. "The Big Count." *Government Executive,* Apr. 1988.

Taeuber, Conrad. "Census." In *International Encyclopedia of Statistics,* edited by William H. Kruskal and Judith M. Tanur. New York: Free Press, Division of the Macmillan Company, 1978.

Thornton, Arland, and Deborah Freedman. "The Changing American Family." *Population Bulletin,* Vol. 38, No. 4, Oct. 1983 (Population Reference Bureau, Washington, D. C.).

"U. S. Population: Where We Are; Where We're Going." *Population Bulletin,* Vol. 37, No. 2, June 1982 (Population Reference Bureau, Washington, D. C.).

Wilkinson, Gary H. "We the Americans." Washington, D. C.: U. S. Bureau of the Census, 1984. (First in a series of reports.)

INDEX